STAR

One Will Always Shine Brighter

To a Very Special friend. Our lives have been trending up since we Met. I'm so excited about our future together

RAPHAEL A. EDWARDS

Disclaimer

1

Contents

Chapter One

They Roar

The crowd went wild when I stepped on to the court with my little sister, Brooklyn sitting on my shoulders. There were a few boos mixed in with all the cheers - but hey, I'm not complaining.

Some might believe that they had good reason to behave like that. But I don't. After all, I am one of the best basketball players of the day. 6 foot 7 inches of pure steel and muscle. I'm good looking, too and I'm a people kinda person. I give my fans a few high fives. Thanks for cheering for the champ. That's right. I'm the top cat in this court. (Did I say I was good looking?).

I love making an entrance on the court with Brooklyn on my shoulders. She's eight years old and adorable. Plus, the crowd loves her almost as much as they love me. I give her a wink as I take her off my shoulders and hand her safely to my friend Mark. She grins and winks back, our little ritual before every game has now been completed.

I shift my attention to Marshall, standing on the court – my best friend, my brother – who plays this game with me. I'm not kidding about the brother part either. We actually tell people that he's my brother. We're always together for every game.

There are 10 seconds on the clock and the other team is up by one point. Marshall starts dribbling the ball and the time seems to stop as the coach starts yelling, *"Marshall, Marshall, run four high, four high!"*

I start getting a sense of déjà vu.

With 10 seconds on the clock, I wipe the sweat off my brow.

"Time to get your head in the game, Darren Drake," I tell myself, "I have the rock, but the shot clock is running out."

With 5 seconds on the clock, I feel the weight of this Pee Wee Championship on my shoulders. I see another boy cutting his way up to the basket and I can feel the pressure release a bit. It's Marshall Goodall. My best friend, reliable and knowledgeable about the game. And he's here.

I can finally move and pass the ball off to Marshall. He makes the lay-up and the crowd goes insane.

Everyone's cheering, and a woman runs on to the court and envelops us both.

My mom's hugs are always the best! Plus, we are still small enough for her to easily wrap her arms around us. As I focus back on the game, the rest is history. As the team lines up, Marshall makes an alley loop pass at me and I make a dunk on someone. I never miss a shot!

We run on the court to celebrate and I can see my mom standing in the corner, clapping and cheering her heart out. A reporter approaches us, and Marshall and I pose. We're still new to the celebrity life but we've already got the million-dollar smile.

I know the picture is going to go with some headline like *"Darren Drake and Marshall Goodall Win Their Fourth PSAL Championship. The Question Now Is: Will They Go Pro or Will They Go to College?* "It's all they have been speculating about.

And to be honest, all I've been thinking about too. We're still little humble stars, after all. As the crowd gets deafening, I can't help but wonder how my life is like a story.

So, let's be a bit cliché here now. My name is Darren, and this is my story. Actually, not so much as *my* story per se but more the story of *our* friendship. Marshall and I. Together, we set the courts ablaze, wherever we played. Some people say we've gotten too big for our boots. At 6 ft 7", I don't think I disagree.

But, before I tell you how we became stars, let us go back to the beginning when playing professionally was only a distant dream and all we wanted was to win for our Pee Wee Championship game.

Chapter Two

○ Patricia's *Little* Problem

My heart sinks again as I scour the stand. It's crowded but I would have still been able to see her if she had come. Yolanda caught my eye and waved happily. I waved back and felt some of the sadness elevate. It was just like the old games. Every time.

Darren's mom would always be on the court, cheering us on and celebrating our wins with us. Patricia, my mother, can never seem to make it. I try to hide my disappointment, but I know Darren can sense it. He follows me into the locker room and asks me in a casual tone.

"So, what's up? You coming to the crib to celebrate?"

"Nah," I reply nonchalantly, "My mom said she got something planned."

I don't know why I lied to Darren. He knows the truth but, sometimes, it is nice to pretend. To hope.

"Cool," Darren replies, "Tomorrow then."

He can sense that I'm not feeling happy and makes one last effort.

"Good game mister! MVP of the game!" he says as he high fives me. I do feel better. I was the MVP, but Darren was better.

"Well, you too Mister. MVP of the league." Darren looks smug but we both grin.

"Now, our hardest decision – college or the league?" I ask.

"I know, right?" Darren says as he high fives me again. We joke about it, but this *is* a really big decision for us.

"I'd get with you tomorrow."

Darren nods and I watch him go out of the locker room. I can see Yolanda and Brooklyn are waiting for him. I can hear them talk and it makes my heart sink again.

"I'm so proud of you Mr. Basketball," she cheers as Darren smiles and hugs her.

"Thanks, Ma."

"Aren't you proud of our brother?" Yolanda asks Brooklyn who smiles and nods yes. Darren picks her up and lets her sit on his shoulders.

"Where's your brother?" she asks Darren and my heart feels full. Yolanda already thinks of me as her son.

"Oh, he's going home tonight. He and his mom have something planned."

Yolanda nods her head and they start walking off.

"Ok, you know it looked like you were having trouble with number 5."

"Yea, so much trouble, he ended up with 11" Darren replies. They laugh as they walk away.

I pick up my gear and start to head towards home. I don't know what to expect. My feet feel like lead, but they still eat up the distance and before I know it, I'm walking in front of my building.

"Another trophy, huh?" a man asks. I look up and then at the trophy in my hand.

"Yep," I reply with a smile.

"Keep doing your thing!" he shouts encouragingly.

"Alright, thanks!" I smile and wave. I feel a bit excited at getting home. Today was a good game and I am MVP. Patricia must have watched the game at least.

I let myself into the house and I can hear the water running in the bathroom.

"Ma…Ma."

As I pass by the bathroom, I can see my mom's boyfriend using the bathroom and he's naked. I scowl angrily and look the other way.

"She's asleep." He calls out to me, but I ignore him and walk into my mom's bedroom. I can see mom lying on the bed. The smell of the room makes it obvious that she's in a drugged-up state. My mom's drug problem is an open secret and she refuses to fix her addiction. It's what has caused her to stick with men like Greg, her current boyfriend.

"Ma…Ma."

As I shake her, I realize she's not just drugged up but also beaten very badly. She can barely open her eyes and one of them is swollen shut. I start to shake her shoulder. When I see her condition, I know. I know she didn't watch the game. I know she was too busy getting her daily fix. I know she was focused only on that. What I don't know is why she was beaten. Why she wasn't able to make Greg happy.

But with Greg, you don't really need a reason. The only thing that keeps the beatings away is drugs. Despite having no money for food, mom's always able to make sure that they get their next fix. Sometimes, getting the drugs don't help either. She's beaten for when there's not enough of the drug, as well.

Greg is a junkie, just like her, but I would say he's even worse. He's prone to anger and violence and any insult, real or not real, is usually answered with his fists. He's beaten my mom up too many times, but she never leaves him or asks him to leave.

"Uhh?" she finally mumbles.

"You okay?" I ask.

"Yeah, I'm fine" she manages to say.

I feel extremely sad and can feel a lump rising in my throat. I fight off my sadness and focus on the positive right now.

"We won, and I got MVP," I say as I show her my trophy. This was the right thing to say as mom makes an effort to sit up.

"Damn, it looks beautiful baby," she exclaims as she tries to grab it out of my hands, "How much do you think we can sell it for?"

Tears roll down my eyes and I have to getaway. I walk out of the room as my mom chuckles to herself.

"Aww! My son about to be in the NBA."

I step out of the building, sit on the stairs and finally cry.

I know it's late, but I have to getaway. I knock on the only door I can, the only place where people welcome me with open arms. Where I am safe enough to cry.

"Don't worry son," Yolanda says as she finally stops hugging me. "Go get some sleep."

I walk into Darren's bedroom where Darren and Brooklyn are sleeping on the bed. I slide Brooklyn forward to make room for myself and lie down. Darren cranes his neck and sees me, throws a pillow at me and goes to sleep.

Chapter Three

PSAL: Going Pro or Going to College

We have both made it into the sacred halls of the Public Schools Athletic League. (PSAL). In fact, the local papers carried the headlines in big bold letters: *"Darren Drake and Marshall Goodall win their fourth PSAL championship. The question now is: Will they go pro or will they go to college"*

This was a really good question and I had no real answer at that point in time. I was kind of hoping that Marshall could help me in coming to a decision. However, he is keeping his cards really close to his chest and won't tell me what he is up to at all.

I head to the press conference with a mixture of anticipation and apprehension. My mind is made up and I know what I have to do with my future. The room is full of reporters and there is pin drop silence when Marshall starts speaking

"Well, I decided that next year I will be attending B.S.U. to play college basketball" he proclaims. For a split second, no one speaks and then everyone starts asking questions. Marshall waves at them and they become quiet. He has that kind of effect on people. I wish I did too. But as my mother hugs him, I say my piece.

"Well, I have decided to enter my name in this year's draft."

And as mom and Marshall stare at me in wonder, I start grinning and tell them I was kidding, "I'm going to B.S.U too!"

For me, it was absolutely inconceivable that I would actually consider doing anything other than what Marshall had in mind. Everyone is laughing and cheering, and little Brookes is jumping up and down for sheer joy, even though she has no idea what is going on. Though I did not know it at the time, this was probably one of the happiest moments in my young life. To this day, when I recollect those tremulous days, I can't help but break out into a grin.

Life at BSU was definitely no walk in the park, regardless of my privileged status.

Chapter Four

○ Life at the BSU

When we left our homes to go to BSU, we had no idea what to expect. This is why our journey was filled with a mixture of apprehension and anticipation with a dash of trepidation.

But we were absolutely determined to do one thing. And that was to rock the world! BSU was the gateway to all our hopes, our dreams, and our wishes.

We had seen the pictures on the website and had seen the videos on YouTube. But nothing had prepared us for the real thing. I mean the place was huge, like really iffin huge. Or maybe it was an average-sized varsity and we had no idea what to expect since we had never been on campus before.

All these thoughts drifted through my mind as assistant coach Hill drove us around the campus. I tried to catch Marshall's eye, but he was too busy ogling the campus to take my words in.

"So over here are the freshman dorms," said assistant coach Hill as he cut through my reverie. I saw this old colonial style building sitting on a small hill.   "So, this is the spot?" I asked. "Not exactly," said coach Hill.

"Actually, since you guys are very special players, we set something else up for you too. That is if you don't mind living with each other." Marshall looked at me and we both looked out of the window of the car. We were suddenly very glad that we will not be sharing a dorm room with other freshmen.

"No problem," said Marshall. "We've been living with each other all our lives," I added. Later on, coach Hill pulled up to a building off-campus.

"Home, sweet home," said the coach

○ Living It Up in The Lap of Luxury

The sight that greeted our eyes was no small freshmen dorm, but an actual 'honest to goodness' luxurious apartment block with state-of-the-art amenities. "This building looks much better than the other one," said Marshall in his typical understated way. "Hell yeah," said coach Hill who was a firm believer in exclaiming his feelings out loud.

I crossed the reception area, waving airily to the receptionist. There was a gold-plated elevator complete with its own operator. I felt slightly self-conscious as I took in his suit and my own jeans, sneakers, and T.

'3rd floor, my good man,' said the coach looking like a man thoroughly enjoying himself. All three of us walked down the elegantly carpeted corridor to our apartment. The coach opened the door and stood aside to let us pass. We walked in and our breath caught in our throats. The place was absolutely beautiful. Worthy of any up and coming yuppie on Wall Street!

We had walked straight into a lavishly furnished living room, with a giant LED TV complete with a 7.1 surround sound system. Soft sofa sets that refused to let you go once you sank into them and a magnificent granite tabletop that looked on to an open yet fully equipped kitchen adjacent to the living room. Even the usually imperturbable Marshall gave a hoop and yelled, "This is so hot!"

I high fived him before flopping down on the sofa. Coach Hill grinned at our enthusiasm and said, "One of the bedrooms has its own bathroom with a Jacuzzi in it." Marshall looked at me and we both ran at the same time. I jumped into the King-sized bed in the room that had the Jacuzzi. "This is mine" I announced with an air of finality.

Marshall jumped right into the bed too. "Well, we are both in here then. I want some tub action too." I started taking off my clothes in preparation for my first every Jacuzzi experience. "That's cool," I said, "because I love to sleep naked and use the bathroom in bed." Marshall aimed a kick at me, but I dodged away laughing at his antics. "Nasty," said Marshall as he flopped on the bed beside me.

Chapter Five

○ The World at Our Fingertips

Afterward, we showered, got dressed, and took the bus that the coach had mentioned. It dropped us at the college gates, and we walked into the rec center. The first thing we noticed was that there were a lot of really good looking women walking around.

A pretty girl caught my eye. "Hey," she waved to us. We bought grinned and waved back. "This is going to be fun," I thought as I high-fived Marshall. Then our thoughts drifted back to the task at hand.

After all, the Uni had not done all this for us for charity alone. They were convinced that we would make waves in the leagues and really make a difference. We both understood that failure was not an option. If we failed to perform, we would be given the boot and we could kiss the scholarships and the fancy apartment goodbye.

○ Meeting the "Don"

A tall stripling young man walked up to me and shook my hand with an iron grip. "Hey, what's up?

I'm the captain, you may call me Don. Coach left a list for the teams. Games are at 7," he said.

The "Don", as we got to know him, was not big on words but showed his passion and his skill through his actions and he wanted everyone else on the team to do the same. A no-nonsense kinda guy and he was fair, but he expected the best from his teammates.

If he thought that anyone else was not giving their best, he would give them a certain number of chances and then talk to the coach about it. This meant curtains for that person's career, at least at BSU.

○ Having Fun, the Old-Fashioned Way

We set the courts on fire and people used to watch us at every turn.

Later on, after a match, as we were heading back Marshall said, "Anyway, I met these chicks in class today, and they having a little party at the crib tonight." "What do they look like?" I asked curiously.

For an answer, Marshall closed his eyes and puts his head back and lets off a loud and long wolf whistle followed by a "Wow!"

"Say no more bro, I got the drift," I replied.

Later on, as I was sitting in the bedroom, Marshall tried on a whole lot of jeans he has bought, but none of them look good to him.

Unlike him, I am not really fussy. So, I pull on the closest pair of pants and T-shirt combo I see. After dressing up, I head to the living room to spend some quality time with our PS 2.

Getting bored, I hollered, "Hey man, come on, by the time you're done, all the cuties will be too liquored up to decide who they really want."

He walks out into the living room in his underwear. "Yo, all my jeans are dirty. Can I borrow a pair of yours?" He asked me. "Oh ho, just go in my room and get some. Just hurry up, so we can bounce," I said, becoming a trifle irritated. "Thanks, dog," he said as he slapped my back and ran past. I got up and turned off the television while yelling, "c' mon lets go, let's go!"

We walk over to the frat house where they are partying for all their worth. In fact, I can actually feel the bass through my body from a full block away. "Maaan is this some shindig or what," Marshall said as he rang the bell.

After the 5th ring, a really pretty girl appeared at the door.

"Hey Marshall!" she said. "Hello, Stacy," he replied.

She gave him a big hug and a resounding kiss on the mouth. Then she looked at me curiously. "Who's this?" She asked. I reached out to shake her hand. "My name's Darren," I introduced myself as I offered her my hand to shake. Much to my amazement, she slapped my hand down and proceeded to hug and kiss me on the mouth too. Not that I minded, of course, but poor Marshall was really confused as he stood behind her shrugging his massive shoulders with a really puzzled look etched on his face.

"Come in. Let's party," said Stacy as she took our hands in hers and dragged us into the frat house. This was my very first party at BSU and I really wanted to make the best of it.

Chapter Six

○ The Party

We walked through the milling crowd. The place was absolutely jam-packed with young men and women energetically grooving to the beat. We decided to get some drinks to fortify ourselves before we took the plunge. Not that it really mattered since we had already made waves and girls were walking by and smiling at us, all the time.

Chris, one of my teammates was talking to a very sexy young lady, but she kept on looking over his shoulder at me. I could see her lips move. "Who's that?" she asked pointing towards me as I waved and smiled at her. "Oh, he is just another freshman on the team who has made his way here from the boondocks in New York," he said in a voice loud enough to reach my ears. "Oh, the Big Apple," said the girl as she stared at me. "Yea, anyway…want something to drink?" asked a visibly disconcerted Chris.

As if waiting for her cue, the minute Chris left, she walked up to me with an airy "hey, how are you doing?"

"I'm alright, and yourself?" I replied. "I'm good now," she says, her eyes now locked on mine as she starts rubbing my stomach and becoming really friendly. "My name's Kimberly, but you may call me Kim," she says. "Err, you know I saw you talking to Chris and I really don't want to step on any toes, man," I said. The last thing I wanted was to pick a fight with a teammate over some chick I had just met.

"Please, I just met him," she said in a dismissive tone. "OK cool," I mumbled as she started gyrating her body over mine.

It was at this point that Marshall decided to walk over. "This is Mmm… Marshall, Marshal Kim" I introduced them. I had difficulty concentrating on what I wanted to say. Kim Stepped back and giggled "Hello Mr. Mmm Marshal, you are cute too!"

Marshall, ever quick on the uptake said, "You know, I heard today is buy one get one free day." "Oh, yea? She smiled, throatily and started to rub Marshall's stomach while continuing to gyrate in front of me. I decided to throw caution to the wind an took her my arms. "What dorm are you guys in?" She asked us both. "We're not in the dorms. We have a condo off-campus." Marshall smiled with his fingers crossed.

Before she could reply Chris comes over with the drinks. He saw her talking and dancing with both of us and was clearly not amused. In fact, he got really upset and slammed the drinks on the table in front of us. A visibly scared Kim finished her drink very quickly indeed. However, the drink clearly fortifies her, and she took a deep breath and said the magic words. "Let's go to your pad." Marshal gave me a broad wink and we head back to our digs where we had an absolutely fantastic time... Together.

○ The End of the Season

Meanwhile, we became an unbeatable outfit and won every match we played. The media loved us, and the papers were full of articles praising 'Darren Drake and Marshall Goodall' for being the driving force behind the B.S.U Pirates' winning streak. The media was not far behind as talk show hosts speculated about our future amidst highlights and snippets of different games in which we had participated and scored.

Finally, we played our heart out for the season's 'Grand Finale.' The issue was never in doubt as both of us blocked and slam dunked our way into the history books. The next day's headlines said it all: "BSU wins it all! What a season!" 'Thanks to

Darren and Marshal's stellar performance' was the byline. The picture showed us holding the championship trophy aloft in our hands. It was a heady moment!

Chapter Seven

The Departure of Greg

After the season ended, we made our way back home. "It's good to be home for the weekend," Marshall said with a long-drawn sigh. "Who you telling, man?" I replied, eager to see my folks again.

"Just come upstairs with me real quick. Let me just drop my bags off." Marshall asked me. I accepted his request and went with him to his pad. We went up to the steps and he unlocked the door.

We were totally unprepared for the sight that greeted our eyes. We found Ma Patricia sitting on the floor, inside the apartment. Her clothes were torn and bloody. She had been beaten very badly and was crying but there were no tears in her eyes. It was as if there were none left anymore.

We rushed into the house together. "Ma...what happened? Just tell us Ma," Marshal was in frenzy, but Patricia seemed to be almost catatonic with shock and refused to even acknowledge his existence. "Was it Greg, huh Ma? Was it Greg?" he persisted.

"Who's Greg?" I asked. "Her punk-ass crackhead boyfriend", he muttered through teeth barely suppressed with rage. He grabbed his mother and started shaking her. "Why did he hit you so bad, Ma?

At last Patricia moaned and answered. "I tried to stop him from pawning your high school MVP trophy." "What? He pawned...he pawned..." words failed Marshall.

○ **The Fight**

Greg chose that moment to walk into the room. He saw us on the floor and sneered, "What the hell are you doing here? Got kicked out of school already, eh? Coming back to live off your poor mother once again?" This was just too much for Marshall who charged at Greg.

They started fighting. Greg tried to kick Marshall in the groin, but he easily sidestepped and went under his fists, only to be met with a rising knee that knocked the wind out of him. "No, stop, please stop" Patricia groaned, but no one listened to her.

By now Marshall was in serious trouble as Greg had pushed him on to the floor and was pummeling him mercilessly. The drugs coursing through his body have made Greg nearly impervious to pain and Marshal's blows simply bounced off him. I can see that Marshall was extremely surprised since he had thought that the older man would be a pushover. I saw the look on Greg's face and realized that there was no stopping him. He was beyond reasoning or control. Marshall did not have much time.

Patricia could not stand to see her only son beaten to death and she runs over to stop Greg. He swatted her away like a fly and she hit her head on the wall and collapsed into a heap, with blood pouring from a fresh wound on her head.

I have had enough and charged Greg and try to push him away from Marshall who was weakly struggling. In return, he delivered a roundhouse to my face that split my cheek open. Something snapped inside me.

I picked him up and slammed him into the ground. It is as if a red mist had descended in front of my eyes. I start punching him relentlessly, all over his body, eventually fixating on his face. I hit him again and again and again. My knuckles were chipped raw and bleeding, but I did not care, I heard bones cracking. I did not care. I saw the blood spurting in fine mists in front of my eyes. I did not care. My eyes, mouth, hands, face, everything was covered in blood. I did not care. Gradually, I realize that Greg is not moving anymore. I look down with dawning horror at the red oozing chuck of meat that was once a human face. I looked at my hands and realize I had done this. Greg will never move again…

"Oh my god, oh my god," I kept saying again and again as Patricia regained consciousness and gave me a hug. Marshall lay unconscious. Somehow, I focused on the gentle cadence of the rise and fall of his chest, to the total exclusion of everything else. The last thing I wanted to focus on, was the body lying next to me.

The next few hours passed by in a blur. I remember nothing from that time. I know Patricia must have called 911. And the EMTs tried to revive Greg. Fat chance!

The police came and took me in for questioning. Mercifully, they did not handcuff me. I was glad for that, especially since the EMTs had bandaged my own wounds and they had now started to sting as the shock wore off.

○ The Trial

I was indicted for 1st-degree manslaughter. From the heights of fame to become a cold-blooded killer who had beaten a man to death with his bare hands – the press had a field day as I tried to come to terms with my newly changed reality.

I was put on trial and I elected to go for a jury of my peers instead of relying on the mercy of a single judge. My attorney showed the jury clippings of my past success as a basketball player. He also presented my trophy that had been shocked by Greg as Exhibit A. After almost three months, the Jury retired to reach a verdict.

I was absolutely terrified with my mouth dry and my heart beating faster than a drum as the jury reassembled in the courtroom. A 'guilty as charged' verdict meant a life in prison.

"Have the members of the jury reached a verdict?" asked the judge. The lead jury member stood up and replied, "We have your honor," and he showed the packed courtroom an envelope. I could not stop myself. "And what is your verdict," I asked the Juror.

By way of an answer, he took the sealed envelope to the judge, who took it from him and tore it open. He took out the piece of paper inside, read it, and put it down. There was pin-drop silence in the courtroom as he paused to sip from a glass of water on the table. The judge cleared his throat and started reading from the piece of paper. Then he stopped and looked at the representative of the jury in an enquiring manner. The man stepped up to the podium and said, "in the case of the state against Darren Drake, we find the defendant not guilty."

For a heartbeat, the pin drop silence continued as the crowd took in the juror's words. Then the room erupted in loud spontaneous cheers. I turned around and hugged both Marshall and his mom in a giant bear hug. We were all in tears, as we walked out of the courtroom.

Later that night, I met Marshall at the local court where we started shooting. This had been our habit for so long that we never became rusty, irrespective of the game season. Once we were done, Marshall asked me the question that was evidently foremost in his mind, "So, what now? You going to try to get into another school?"

"Nah, I'm out. I got me a gig in Italy. So, I'm out in a day or two." I replied. It was the truth, especially since I had been thinking of nothing but my career for the past couple of months or so.

We walked over to the bleachers and sat down. "I just wanted to tell you thanks for protecting my mom, you know..." Marshall's voice's traced off. "Come on man, you are like my brother, I love you," I said before he could continue. "I love you too, man. Do your thing out there. And call me as soon as you get stable." He said, his voice breaking as if there was a great big lump inside his throat. We stood up and hugged and went on our way.

The next day mom and little Brooklyn came with me to the airport to drop me off. Marshall had disappeared.

"Are you going for the draft too, like Marshall?" 5-year-old Brooks asked me, even though she had little idea what the draft even meant. "No, not yet. But soon." I replied.

"So, I'll see you later. Do your thing out there. No, matter what happens, just do what you do best. Don't worry about us. We'll be fine," mom said as she leaned over and kissed me on the forehead.

"I love you son."

"I love you too Ma. And you too, Brooks."

I tickled Brooks under her face. She giggled and grabbed me in a hug. I responded by sweeping her off her feet and putting her on my shoulders, one last time. "Brooks you are getting heavy, I won't be able to do this for long," I said, pretending to sag under her weight. Her giggles turned to squeals of laughter. They were sweet music to my ears.

Chapter Eight

○ I Am Off to Italy

Time passed quickly. More than three months passed since I landed in Italy to do what I do best. And that is play basketball.

But it was not like playing at home. Not by a long shot (pun intended). Yes, I scored and played very well, but I was not really good enough. It seemed that nothing I did was really good enough for my Italian teammates.

Once as I was jockeying in position for a lay-up in a practice game, one of the forwards on the other team fouled me hard. I landed in a heap on the floor. I could feel the copper taste of my own blood from a cut lip. I was bleeding badly. "Damn," I mumbled as I slowly got up, only to see the rest of the team just walk away like they really did not give a damn.

As I walked over to the locker room, I saw my coach Luigi standing beside the door, "Drake...you alright?"

"Yes," I nod back, picking up an icepack from the fridge. "Come on then, let's finish the practice." He said totally ignoring my condition. I wiped away a smear of blood from my mouth, squared my shoulders and ran right back onto the court. We continued our practice. The two teams went back and forth for a while.

Then a fellow team member named Antonio got hit on his hand. It was a slight sprain as he fell and landed on his hand. The rest of the team ran over to him with a sense of extreme urgency. They started asking him in Italian if he was OK. Meanwhile, coach Luigi looked really worried. So much so that he called out in English. "Ok, enough practice for today!"

○   The Practice Session

I was absolutely flabbergasted that the coach would just end practice like this. I was primed that I decided to let off steam by shooting some free-throws. Meanwhile, Antonio joined me after a little while.

"You ok?" I asked him. "Yea, I'm fine. Just didn't want to practice anymore." He replied. I started grinning at the whole unfairness of it all. "Dude... The big fella knocked me to the floor, and it was just whatever. You get hit on your finger and it's the end of the world. You must've been playing with these guys for years, eh?" I surmised.

This time it was Antonio's turn to start laughing as he shook his head. "Naah man, I just got on the team just this year only." My jaw dropped, "For real?"

"See it's like this," Antonio explained, "You're a very good player Drake. But you're not Italian." He gave me a knowing wink and walked away, leaving me to stare at his retreating back.

○ The Draft

A couple of months later, I take out time from a hectic practice session to watch the annual NBA draft on TV at my home. The announcer said, "Anndddd the fourth pick in the draft: Marshall Goodall from BSU has been selected by the Chicago Bulls."

The Bulls are one heck of a maverick outfit. I can't help it. I yell and dance around to release my pent up energy. I know that mom and Brooklyn are also watching the draft right along with Marshall's mom, Patricia.

I must have tried to call my bro a dozen times. But I keep getting voicemail only.

Undeterred, I decided to leave a message "Congratulations boy! I am going to be at home, and we will paint the town red! Then get you ready for that league. Call me when you get this. Not too late though, I got a game tomorrow."

Struggling in Rome

I was not kidding; I really had a big game the next day. I was up against a top-level Italian team. But my concentration was shot to hell and back. I simply could not get over the fact that my own team did not care about me at all. I knew I was struggling, and the perennially sneering expressions of my teammates and their snide remarks in Italian were messing up my game big time. The more frustrated I got, the more shots I missed.

When the final horn blew, I looked up and saw the scoreboard. It showed 100 to 80. My team had lost. The whole team blamed it on me, and I got many unkind jostles and pushes as I went to the locker room. I wanted to go and drink, but I didn't want to do it alone and there was no one else I knew in this city. So, I went back home.

I struggled with myself a bit, but I was too lonely to care. I called my mother. "I am telling you Ma; one more bad game and I am finished out here."

I was too upset to hear the weakness in her voice or to understand the true grim reason behind her hacking coughs. "My boy, you're averaging 22 points a game and they want to send you home?" She asked. " Ma I'm telling you; they don't play that out here. I can't afford to get sent home, we need the money ma."

"Son, basketball doesn't define you. I mean, you do that best but there's so much more to Darren Drake. Believe me, son, you're great whether you're out there playing ball or not. You have the world at your fingertips."

I mulled over her words. They made me feel a bit better. "Thanks, ma. Anyway, how's Marshall?"

Her reply left me a bit surprised, "I don't know son, I haven't heard from him since you left."

"Really? Ah well, he might be really busy in Chicago." I said more to myself than her. This time her prolonged coughing fit got my attention. "You ok, ma?" I asked, "Yea, I'm fine, I just have a little cold." My mom was one hell of a good liar. "Alright, then kiss Brook for me. I love you guys."

"I love you too baby. And when you talk to Marshall, tell him to come over here and see his mother." When was the last time you spoke to him?" I was on a spot and I knew it.

"Umm, last night", I lied.

"Ok, baby, I love you," she said as she hung up.

I sat in the dark with my phone in my hand for a long time. I tried calling Marshall again and I still got his damned voicemail!

"I know you're busy, dog, but I haven't talked to you since I been out here. CALL ME." I almost shouted out the last two words in my frustration. I threw the phone on the sofa and went to take a shower.

Chapter Nine

○ Patricia Goes Home

Next day I stayed at home to watch the Chicago Bulls game. Marshall seemed to be doing ok when my phone started to ring.

"Hello," I said. It was Luigi, my Italian coach. "Hey Darren, he. "Hey, coach" I replied. "Your best friend is playing." "I know, I'm watching the game, Luigi."

"He is good. But not as good as you, Darren." The coach seemed to be picking his words with care. "Hmm," I grunted noncommittally to draw him out.

"Tomorrow, come to the gym early. I have a scout from the Nuggets that wants to speak to you." He said. I sat up in the bed with my heart beating fast with excitement. 'Ok, coach.' Catch you tomorrow." I could barely contain my excitement as I put my phone down. I went to the washroom to cool off with a badly needed shower. Yesssssss! My gamble at missing the draft and coming to Italy seems to be paying off, finally!

My phone rings again and I ran back into the bedroom.   "Yea?" "Is this Darren Drake?" I recognize Dr. Edmond's voice. "Yes." "Darren, I'm sorry to tell you this, but your mother passed away late last night."

I could not breathe. It seemed as if the floor has swallowed me whole. I don't remember dropping the phone, don't remember the rest of the doctor's words. My mind, unable to bear the calamity of the loss, had simply deleted those few minutes from my memory.

Patricia's Funeral

I could hear somber music playing in the background as I sat with little Brooklyn in my lap at the Church where we were holding Mother's wake. Each time the church door opened, I would turn to see who was coming in to pay their respects. I could see the people in the church were in tears. In fact, their tears were gushing as the preacher gave the sermon.

I was dry-eyed. Perhaps I had yet to come to grips with the shock, to understand that Ma was gone, forever. I kept looking at my right side, waiting for my brother, my friend Marshall. But all I could see was a stranger staring right back at me.

Soon, the sermon ended and everyone I gave me their condolences. Once the church was empty, uncle Rich ushered me and Brooks into his car and took us home.

Later, as we sat at the dinner table, he asked me, "so, what are you planning to do for money? I know the funeral kinda set you back a bit." "Not sure yet," I replied. It was the truth. I had not even thought about money issues since I heard the news of my mother's death.

"I really don't have any money to lend you, but if you want, Brooklyn can stay with me." Uncle Rich offered. Brooklyn shook her head violently in an empathic "no" while grabbing onto my arm as tightly as she could. "Nah uncle, that's cool. I... I will figure something out." I said, with a confidence I did not feel.

At that moment, the doorbell rang and the man that had kept staring at me at the church walked over to the dinner table. "Excuse me, I don't mean to interrupt, but I just wanted to give my condolences." He said. "Thanks a lot, man" I reached out to shake his hand. "Who are you?" I asked. " Oh, my name is Kevin. We went to high school together. Do you remember?" "Umm yeah,

yeah I do. Thanks, man." I said without the vaguest idea as to who he was.

"That was nice." Uncle Rich said, once Kevin was gone. I nodded my head in affirmation. "I say, Darren, what about your best friend Marshall? I mean, where is he?" Asked Uncle Rich. "Marsh Marsh." Chimed in little Brooks.

I say, isn't he in the NBA now? Can't he help you?" Uncle queried. I looked him in the eye and just shrugged my shoulders.

○ Looking for Work

The next day I work up early in the morning to look for work. My mom did not have any savings. Since she was not insured, what little she had was wiped out by the medical bills. My own stash was spent taking care of the funeral.

I sat on the floor busy highlighting parts of the help wanted section of the classifieds in the newspaper. Brooklyn sat with me eating cereal and watching television. I shortlisted the ads I wanted to apply and went for at least four interviews that first day. All of the prospective employers turned me down. Apparently, there was no demand for ex-basketball players in the job market.

The days turned to weeks and now some cereal was all that was left in the fridge. I tried out for the lowest blue collar jobs I could find, but nothing worked out for me at all.

Chapter Ten

○ Life at the Local YMCA

Soon, I had to make a decision. To stay at my mom's house, or to go to the local YMCA branch. It was a no-brainer. The choice was sitting at home and starving or seeking charity. My pride may have stopped me from looking for handouts, but I had little Brooks to think about.

So we rolled up our meager possessions and walked into the YMCA (Young Men Cristian Association) building. We were allotted two small beds and a pillow each. As I was fixing the beds, I saw that a bunch of homeless people was sleeping on the bare floor in the gym.

At least we had beds of our own. I hugged Brooks tightly as we tried to sleep. Sleep did not come easily, those first few nights.

I used to lie on the bed with Brooklyn lying on my chest. "I wanna go home…I wanna go home…" She used to wail. I tried to rock her to sleep even as my eyes started to water of their own accord. I wish dad was here. It was bad enough to survive on handouts alone, but for my baby sis to the do the same. It was just too much to bear. "We will baby…in a couple of days, we will go back home." I used to reassure her. Thank goodness, it was always too dark for her to see my own tears.

One day, as I walked by the TV, I stopped to see the Chicago Bulls playing on their home turf. The commentator said, "This kid, Marshall Goodall is a great player. He's going to be around for a while." I had long since stopped trying to get in touch with him.

It had been over a month since we had shifted to the YMCA and I was still looking for work. One evening as I walked into the main YMCA dorm. I caught a waft of the most pungent odor I ever had the misfortune to smell. It was uniquely terrible, and I thought I was going to gag. "Woo! What's that smell?" I asked Brooks who was holding her nose. A homeless man answered me. "The rice…it's plum rotten." Brooks tugged at my leg. "I'm hungry DD." I took a deep breath, promised her I would be back with some food and walked out of the building.

○ The Chase

I leaned against a car outside a Chinese fast-food restaurant. I could smell the delectable aroma of

Chop Suey and fried rice. I remember just staring in a daze at the place. Thinking of Brooks gnawing hunger.

I was then I saw a man walk out with a big bag of food. As the man walked ahead of me, I darted out, grabbed the bag and took off, running as fast as my athletic body could carry me. "Stop thief...Police!!" Yelled the freshly dispossessed man, who saw his meal disappearing down the road.

I had expected that, and I was not overly concerned since he was too fat to give chase. However, there was a problem. A police officer across the street saw what had happened and he started chasing me too. This was not good. Definitely not good at all!

"Stooooppp"! Yelled the cop. I picked up my pace and really took off, even as the police officer continued running after me.

My mind went back to the time when Marshall and I were young kids and how we loved to race. I remembered Marshall's mom going "On your mark, get set, go." As we ran and ran and ran...

I was bought out of my reverie by a loud bang and something whizzing past me. I turned back and was aghast with shock. The cop had his Glock 17 out and had just tried to shoot me! I ducked into a side alley and quickly lost the cop.

It was night by the time I made it back to the YMCA. "Here baby, I got you some food," I said as I woke her from her slumber. Brooklyn smiled. "Thank you, DD, I love you." "I love you too, baby," I said as I played with her hair as she ate her meal.

The Chance Meeting

I walked by a sneaker store peering in to see if there was a 'help wanted' sign in the window. There wasn't, but I really wanted to go inside and ask if they would hire me for anything. A man walked out and looked at me and my old and dusty clothes. "Hey, we're closed…You hear me, kid?" he said. "I know, all of you guys are closed, the minute you see me," I replied bitterly.

He looked at me again a bit closer, this time. "Hey. You are Darren Drake, aren't you?" I nodded my head. The next thing I knew, the man was shaking my hand enthusiastically. "Hey, I used to watch you play in high school. You're damn good. How you been?" he gushed.

"I'm alright," I mumble. "So what, you still playing or what? What you doing, man?"

"Well actually, I'm looking for a job," I confessed.

Joe looked a bit confused at my confession. But he rallied with an, "Ok, give me your number. Maybe I can help."

"I don't have a number. My sister and I are at the YMCA." I could not look him in the eye. He looked a bit disappointed. "As a matter of fact, I have something here for you," he said, "If you want, I have a furnished apartment upstairs for rent. You and your little sister can stay there."

I started smiling as if a great load had been taken off my back. "When do I start?" I asked. "Come tomorrow at nine." He answered, shaking my hand with his prodigious one. "Thanks a lot, dude."

As I am getting ready to run off. He called me back "Hey…Hey come here, don't you want the key to upstairs?" "Umm now?" I asked.

"Yea, you and your sister don't deserve to stay in a YMCA," he said. "But, I can't pay you yet," I protested. "Don't worry. After you save up some money, then I'll start to charge." He replied. I shook my head and accepted the keys in mute gratitude.

Chapter Eleven

○ Joe and Kevin

Meanwhile, unbeknownst to me Joe had flashbacks of his own. His remembered sitting in the stands with his son at one of my high school games. He watched me as I dribbled and weaved my way through the opposing team to score... Again and again.

It was at that point in time that he had hugged his son and said   "See that kid? He's going to be a special player in the league someday."

It was a particularly memorable game. As he told me all about it, I remembered it as well. He saw me step back and hit a jump shot from the deep end. And he was watching intensely even when I stuck out my tongue at Marshall and gave him a quick high five. "So easy, look at how he scores." Joe had mumbled to his son, in those far off halcyon days.

○ Life as A Shoe Store Helper

The next day, I came to work early in the morning and helped as many customers as I could. Looking at people's feet was way different from my days playing basketball. But I had a sister to think of and there was no room for self-pity. In fact, if anything, I was grateful for earning my own keep and making sure that my baby sis could afford to go to school and eat properly.

Meanwhile, I figured out that Joe was something of a basketball fanatic. He would sit in the back of the store watching television all day long, oblivious to his customers. Once he got so excited that he started yelling at the screen. "Shoot the ball when you're open. Uhhh! Those damn kids." Needless to say, the customer I was helping, was quite startled.

As I started to walk towards the back of the store one day, I met Kevin. "Yo, Darren Drake. When you started working here?" I was a bit a puzzled as he shook my hand. "Kevin, remember? I came to your mom's funeral." He explained. "Oh yea, yea. What's up?" I said as the light or recollection dawned in my mind. "I need a shoe that's gonna give me the most rise on my bounce." He said. "The most rise, huh?" I could not help giggling and offered him a pair. "What about these?"

"Yea, these are hot, but will they help me get up?" he said. "I think so," I replied. He became serious.

"So, D, let me ask you a question. How come that bum Marshall made it and you didn't?" I shrugged my shoulders with a serious expression on my face. "I don't know. Right place at the right time."

"Oh well, it doesn't matter anyway, cause you guys are like brothers. I know he takes care of you very well…right?"

I could not look him in the eye, so I change the subject. Marshall's very name made me feel all hot and bothered. "Umm right, what size you need in this?" I asked. "Nine and a half." He replied. As I walked back into the storeroom to get the desired size, Kevin went to talk to Joe. "Hey, Joey, what's up?" I heard him ask.

Joe punched Kevin in the arm, hard "Owww! What was that for man?" He yelled in outraged anger. "Takes care of him so well, he has to work here," said Joe. "Sorry man, I didn't know." He replied.

I came back with the shoes and Joe and Kevin stopped talking. "Here you go," I said. Kevin tried them on. They were a perfect fit and he leaned over and gave Joe the money. "Thanks, dude," he said to Joe and shook his hand.

"Why don't you play ball with us after work?" He asked me. "Nah, I'm cool," I replied. He gave a disbelieving snort. "You're cool? What, you retired at the age of 23?" "Look, I don't feel like it. Ok." I said a tad testily. "All right, all right, I'll see you later," said Kevin.

"You know if you wanna go later, my daughter can watch Brook," Offered Joe. "I don't want to play. But I can go do something a little later if she doesn't mind watching her." I told him. "No problem," said Joe.

Later that day I took the opportunity to go to the park by myself and just shoot a few hoops around. I had not lost my touch and I was scoring every jump shot that I took. My different dribbling moves and techniques were still pretty rad, and I could score whenever I wanted.

The Arrival of Mr. Vann

I saw an old man sitting by the chess table in the park, watching my moves. It had been a long time I had an audience, so I took a long shot and scored. "Nice, right?" the old man waved at me in a dismissive gesture. "You ain't nothing, kid." I laughed and then hit another crack shot.

Later on, as I was walking home, I saw a crowd around the park. When I got closer, I saw a whole bunch of people playing basketball pick-up. These guys were dunking and hitting shots while doing fancy dribble moves. Kevin was also amongst them. When he saw me ran over to talk to me. "What's up,dude? You come to play, huh? We go next."

"I'm good," I said as I jogged off, dribbling my ball.

When I got back to Joe's home, I picked up a sleeping Brooklyn from upstairs. Thanked his daughter and carried the child back to the downstairs apartment. I put the covers over Brooklyn and kissed her on the forehead. Then I walked into the dingy little living room, lay down on the couch, and turned on the television. My mind was blank as I shifted the channels.

The next day in the store I caught a bit of TV time with Joe before we opened. Kevin walked into the store as we were watching a baseball game. "Hey, Joe," he called. "Yes," Joe answered back.

"You know, you're the fattest Jew in Brooklyn." All of us start laughing. "Hey, Kev, are you getting taller?" jibed Joe. "Ohhh! That gonna hurt," I said since Kevin was a bit short and really sensitive about his height. "That wasn't funny," he retorted.

Kevin looked over to the wall where we had placed our all-new line of sports sneakers. "Hey, when did you get all these, man?" Kevin said as he picked up a pair of StreetGodz shoes. "They were on backorder and we just got them in," I replied. "Good move fat boy. These are hot!" Kevin said to Joe.

"Anyway, why you didn't stay and ball with us last night?" he asked us both. "Maybe 'cause you can't ball," replied Joe. "Nah, I was shooting up the block and I was kinda tired. Next time," I said. "Next time you go to work on your game, call me, I'll come to shoot with you. My jay could use a little work," Kevin said.

Joe giggled as Kevin gave him a dirty look. "Anyway, I'm going to Club Blue tonight. Wanna rock?" Kevin asked me. "I'm good. I don't have anyone to watch Brooklyn."

"You can get her from upstairs when you get back," Joe offered. I really did not want to impose on anyone, and I guess it showed on my face. "Come on, it's gonna be hot!" he urged. "Oh alright." I relented. It was never a good idea to push one's friends away after all.

As I got up to help a customer. Kevin went, "Yo!Chicago's in town tomorrow. Can you get tickets from your boy?" I heard Joe take a deep breath. I kept my cool and replied, "Nah, I don't think so."

As I walked away I heard Kevin ask Joe, "What's up with him?"

"I think they had a bad falling-out. He doesn't talk about it much. If I were you, I wouldn't either." I heard Joe reply to Kevin. "Ah well, no skin off my back mate," said Kevin as he started looking around the store. He noticed that Joe has a lot of different uniform jerseys for sale. "Hey, man," he said tapping Joe on the shoulder. Why you start selling all these silly jerseys?"

"Gotta take advantage of all your brothers and homeboys." Laughed Joe. Two young boys walked over to Joe. "Hey, how much for that Kobe Jersey?" the younger of the two asked Joe. "For you, give me one hundred." As the kid dug out his wallet from his pocket, Kevin said, "Hey shorty, don't get that. The Lakers about to trade him then you gonna be stuck with that garbage."

"You know, that's right. Thanks, man." And he walked out of the store with his friend. Kevin mimicked Joe as he had laughed earlier. Joe put up his middle finger and I went back to work after watching this little tableau.

"I'll pick you up around 11," said Kevin as he passed by me on his way to the exit.

⊙ The Night Out

Later that night as I was standing in front of the store, Kevin pulled up in a shiny new all black Range Rover. "Woo!" I said as I got into the truck and slapped Kevin a high five. "This is you, man?" I asked

"Nah, it's one of my bros," he replied. "Damn, one of...what? He in the league, he ballin?" I queried. "Yea, he ballin, just not like you." "Oh, ok," I shook my head as we drove off.

"Ok. You got a fresh pair of whites, air force ones," said Kevin, checking out my footwear. "Oh, these. I needed em, I call these my cocaines." "Cool name bro," laughed Kevin.

The club was throbbing with some really cool music. And it was absolutely jampacked with people. I roved my eyes over all the really good looking women in there as Kevin passed me a drink. "It's crazy in here, right?" he asked me. I shook my head in disbelief.

"In a word: WOW," I said. "So now what? You gonna get something outta here?" he asked me. "Maybe...Maybe." I replied as the crowd started moving in a body towards the door. "Who's that? "I asked. "Somebody famous, the way all them chickens running over there," Kevin replied.

It was then that it happened. The DJ made an announcement. "Ohhh boy! It's heating up tonight. We have Marshall Goodall in here. What's up, baby?" And I saw Marshall walking through the crowd flanked by his security detail.

It was as if time had frozen for me. "You wanna get out here?" Asked Kevin. "Naah I'm good," I replied mechanically. For me, everything was happening in grotesque show motion.

o   The Long Overdue Meeting

Marshall was surrounded by a lot of women who have been waiting for him. He was too busy signing autographs to even see me. In fact, he walked right next to me when he saw I was there. He just shrugged his shoulder with a "whatever" expression on his face. He tried to slap me a high five. But I refuse to extend my hand.

"Hey, Darren, what's up?"

As if nothing had happened. I just stared at him and slowly shook my head. "Hey, dog, I got your message, I just been really busy with the season and other things", he tried to explain.

But even this explanation was punctuated with a girl pushing him. "Come on baby, I'm ready to drink. "She told him. I looked at the girl until she got uncomfortable. "...and other things,"I said with a deadpan expression.

"Oh, yea, I'm sorry about your mom too, ok." He did not sound sorry at all.

"My mom... For 19 years, she was your mom too Nigga," I replied, my voice thick with rage.

"So what now? Do you want money or something? I'm supposed to take care of you? Here take it. Take it all." Marshall took out a large stack of hundreds and peeled some bills off. He put them on the bar next to my chair.

"Look, things are just different now. I mean, when we were younger, that buddy-buddy thing was cool. Now, I'm just on a higher level." He gave me a peace sign that I did not return. "Stay up, baby!" He said before he walked off. I took the money and handed it to the waitress. "Here you go, baby," I said, mimicking Marshall. The waitress smiled her gratitude.

"Let's get out of here," I told Kevin. As we walked outside the club to his Range Rover, my emotions got the better of me and I pick up an empty bottle from the street and threw it as far as I could in a bid to curtail my raw fury.

"What's up with you two?" A visibly alarmed Kevin asked me. I ignored him and just leaned on the car with a heavy sigh. "What is it? You mad cause he in the league and you not. Is that it?" I just rolled my eyes and gave him a sarcastic look.

"What you mad cause he got paper now? The man is rich. He's not the same person you grew up with. Maybe he deserves to be there a little more than you." That hurt big time. "Look at me...you ever see me do my thing on that court?"

This time it was his turn to nod his head in a sarcastic 'yes'. "Dude. I am a star. Me not having money, cars or women will never change that." I mumbled more to myself than him. "Seems like just yesterday we were in college together. From one day to the next, cause of a little money, everything just changes, huh?" I started yelling in sheer frustration. "I'm the nicest cat in the league. And I'm not in the league." I said bitterly! "You all right." Asked a visibly perturbed Kevin.

"The worst thing is, yea, he played me. We've been together since we were five years old. But damn, how you don't come to the funeral of the only woman that took care of you and loved you." I could not stop the tears from welling into my eyes as I looked over at Kevin. "My mom used to wash this dude's drawers. If I had one plate of food, it was split between the both of us, and you don't come to the funeral?"

We both got into the Rover. I sit back in my seat and put my hands over my eyes. "I don't know, man. I just don't know." Muttered Kevin.

The next day in the store, Kevin came over and Joe and I took a break to sitin the back and watch some TV.

"Hey, I was talking to a buddy of mine who's a pretty good agent. He says he remembers you and would love to help you out this summer." Said Joe. "That's what I mean baby, a look. A legit look. When do you go to camp, Joe?" Kevin jumped up and down excitedly.

"Hey, listen up, I'm talking to the kid over there." Joe giggled as he pointed at me. "Thanks, Joe. That'll be cool." I replied. "Just let me know what summer leagues you're going to be playing in, so we can come to watch," said Joe. "That's cool," I repeated.

"Hey, I'm glad I was able to give you guys a good chuckle," Kevin said as I grabbed his head in a vise lock.

"Come on man, you know it wasn't like that. You gonna come shoot with me tonight?" I said. "Hell yeah, what time?" he inquired. "When I get off," I replied. "Ok then, I'm going to leave now so I can ice up." He said as he walked out. I looked at my watch. It was 3:00 PM. "I'm going to take my lunch break," I said. A talent scout was not someone to be taken for granted after all.

"You're gonna pick up Brook?" Joe asked as I walked towards the door. "Yes," I called out as I grabbed a basketball off of the shelf. "Make sure you start practicing, Darren." "Don't worry about me, Joe. You just put the agent in the seat." I said dribbling the ball through my legs. I shot it at the rim. It went in smoothly. "And I'll put the ball in the bucket," I finished.

I went to Brooklyn's school and waited for the teacher to bring her downstairs. When Brooklyn saw me, her face lit up in a smile and she ran towards me. "DD, DD," she yelled. I picked her up and gave her a hug and a kiss. "Hey young lady, how was school today?" I asked as I picked her up and placed her on my shoulders. "Goooooooood," she sang.

"So, what did you do today? " I read," she answered.

"What else?" "I ate."

"What else?" "I Slept."

We were both giggling by this time. "What else?" I said tickling her as she sat on my shoulder. "Well, what else?" I said in mock anger. "And I readdddd."

"Ok, so you had a good day, eh?" She nodded her head enthusiastically as we walked into the apartment. "Home, sweet home. Brooklyn." But to my surprise, she started crying and shaking her head "no." "I wanna go home.""We are home, baby," I tried to console her. "No, home where mommy lives. I want my mommy DD.""I do too...I do too, baby." I said as I rocked her to sleep.

Playing the Game with Kevin

Later that night, I met Kevin in the park as I had promised. I ran with the ball from one end of the court to the other as I touched the line, then I ran back. Kevin passed me the ball. I did a complex dribble move, then shot the ball right into the basket. I did this about three more times.

Meanwhile, out of the corner of my eye, I saw that Vann, the old man that was in the park the other night. He was there again, watching me. "Damn, are you gonna miss one? This is getting monotonous," said a visibly peeved Kevin.

"Oh please!" yelled out to Vann. "You need to watch out pops," said Kevin as I stopped shooting.

"That's the old man that told me I was garbage the other night," I told Kevin.

"You're not," said Vann.

Kevin started to laugh at Vann's serious expression. "Who have you seen in the past three years that's better?" I challenged.

"You...one year ago. But even then, your handle was suspect. But at least you had some fire in your eyes." Vann said, looking me in the eye. I exchanged looks with Kevin.

"Pops is bugging," I said. "He's been hitting on Grandma too much. Grand Marnier, that is." Said Kevin as he started to laugh. "What you said, boy? I never had a drink in my life." Said Vann. Looking at me again.

"How you young cats say it? Real is real? I could give you a handle and put that fire back in your belly. And that's real," he challenged. "A handle? You see how I shoot this thing?" I retorted, even as I took a shot from far out and it went straight in. "Big deal. A fat white boy can stand up and make every shot." He then imitated how I was running and shooting on the move. "So when you start moving and doing that, you'll become a beast," he said.

The dude knew his game for sure. I decided to listen to him and follow his advice. "When do we start?" I asked eagerly. He just smiled and walked away. "Tomorrow night." He called.

"Hey, little man, you bring a rock too. Might as well learn something." He told Kevin who was hanging on to his every word. "No number I could call you at?" I called after him. "I'll be out here when you get here," He said as he walked away.

Chapter Twelve

Learning the Ropes from the Old Man

Next day, I walked into the park with Kevin. "I want to get Pops on the court and bust his butt," said Kevin. I could not help laughing at his enthusiasm. "He's like fifty-something years old," I replied. "So what, he talks big trash." Said Kevin.

'Bout time you got here. Shorty what's up? Come on, we got a lot of work to do," said Vann walking onto the court.

"See what I'm talking about?" Kevin mumbled in an undertone.

"See, your problem is you have no enthusiasm for the game. No fire. And your handle is soft," said Vann. Kevin failed to suppress a giggle even as he gave Vann the ball. "I want you to back-peddle and throw the ball between your legs. When you get to half court, come back with a cross over, and take your shot. On every shot, I want you to yell, "ahhhh," ok?" Instructed Vann. "Sure," I said as I took the proffered ball from him.

"Let me hear from you," he said.

"Eh, hear me what?" I was confused. "Yell!" Vann opened his eyes wide and let loose with an, "ahhhh!" I laughed and also yelled "Ahh." "Yell like a man, son. Ahh!" said an unimpressed Vann. "Ahhh," I gave it my all. "Yea, like that. Now, let's go, go, go!" said Vann.

As we were about to start the drill, Kevin yelled behind Vann's back, "Ahhh!" Vann was startled. Kevin started laughing.

We started the game. I back-peddled and dribbled the ball. But somehow, I could not quite get into the spirit of the game I loved so much. I kept losing it. "No, no boy. Move!" Vann said as he started wiggling his head and his shoulders. "Get a beat to your dribble – you should sound like – Bump, bump, bump. My dribble sounds like a bump, bap, bap, bump, bap – come on, pick up the pace."

I tried it as he showed me. "Ok. Cross 'em up shoot." I did and forgot to yell. "What happened to my, Ahhhh!" Said Vann. "Ahhhh!" I yelled dutifully.

"Alright, don't forget it again," he said as we continued to practice.

As time passed, both of us continued to drill with Mr. Vann. Eventually, Van just became a simple spectator. I became as fluid as water under Vann's able tutelage. I would cross, dunk, and shoot and yell... Always that yell! It became the hallmark of my game.

○ Meanwhile in The Major Leagues

Unknown to me, two league fire boys called Rob and Derrick (Kevin's elder brother) had an argument in the VIP section of a really posh bar. "Some of those cats in the league are garbage. I'm telling you, I know a kid named Flight up north, that's better than half the league," said Derrick drinking his champagne.

Kevin walked up to them. "What's up?" He slapped both Derrick and Rob a high five. "Ask my brother," said Derrick.

"Eh, What?"said Kevin. "See Kev Boy, a lot of them dudes in the league are soft right?

"Soft as wet bread. Man" Replied Kevin. They all start laughing after that.

"Well, I haven't seen any straight-up street ballers that can hang," said Rob. "That can hang...what the... If my man Darren was in the league, he would lead it in scoring," replied Kevin. "What? He nice like that?" asked Rob.

"Nice. That's the understatement of the year dude!" Kevin reported.

"Why I never heard of him?" Asked Rob again. "You have, remember that cat who beat the body charge last year?" Chipped in Derrick. "Oh yeah, that's your man," said Rob. Kevin shook his head, "Yes."

"Dude, that's what I mean. There's a lot of cats like that," said Derrick.

The Street Vs. the League

"We should have a one-on-one tournament. The street versus the league," said Kevin.

"Oooohhh, that will be so hot," said Rob. "Yea, we can get a sneaker company to sponsor everything," said Kevin, warming up to the idea.

Derrick took a sip from his drink. "We should, right?"

The months passed as the idea took hold. Meanwhile, Kevin and the Derrick and Rob duo got into action to make sure that there were no hitches. It was a new thing and it had never been attempted before.

One day, as I was fixing some boxes in the back of the store, Kevin ran right in looking very excited.

"Hey Joe, where's the kid?" He asked.

Joe pointed towards the back while reading his newspaper. I was on the ladder when he just grabbed my leg. I was very startled and fell on top of all of the boxes. I was really upset since I could have been hurt bad. Darren gets up looking upset. "What the…"

"My fault, dog. Listen, my brother and couple of his boys are gonna have a tournament."

"I really don't want to play in no rinky-dink league," I said as we walked out to the front of the store. "Rinky-dink, huh?" He said. "Yea" I retorted.

"For their rinky-dink tournament, they scratched up a million dollars for the winner. So take that and snort it Mr. High and mighty," he said.

Joe was not the only one surprised. "One Million! Hell no!" I yelled. "I told you, they got cake," said Kevin. I needed to sit down, my heart was beating so fast. "Damn, hell yea. I'm gonna play!" I said.

Kevin told me all about it. I was really enthusiastic. Not only was I ready to go, but all those training sessions with Mr. Vann had honed my skills to the proverbial razor's edge.

"Play? You better win, and I can get the StreetGodz Company to back the event," said Joe.

"Definitely, who's more of a Streetgod than you. The kids in the neighborhood love you and you dominate on that court. You're a neighborhood god, all your peers that never made it respect you and the little ones look up to you. It would be no problem."

"So that's what's up," said Kevin. "And my brother could add to whatever the put is," he finished. "Me!?!" I pointed at myself. "No ole Joe here...Yeah, you! And his boy Rob put up the rest on any one of the NBA cats to win," said Kevin.

"I don't understand." I really didn't. I just thought it was going to be a regular game.

"It's a one-on-one tournament. Eight of the best NBA cats against eight of the best street ballers. Some real Gladiator-type games."

"Who are the cats from the league?" I asked.

"What difference does it make? Are you down?"

"Hell yeah!"

This was my big chance and I would be damned if I miss it. "My man, I'll see you tonight in the park," said Kevin as he punched my shoulder.

"One million...You think you can win?" Asked Joe. He looked as dazed as I felt. "Hell yeah," I replied.

The local channels were having a field day. It seems that every time I switched channels, there was the same announcement.

"Hello to all our viewers. We have so much to talk about tonight, but first, we start in NYC where a private charity has planned to put up one million dollars for the Boys & Girls Club of America. It's for a one-on-one basketball tournament. Eight street ballers and eight NBA ballers meet like Gladiators 'til there's only one. Woo! The eight NBA players are Steven Bradford, Luke Bond, Alex Whitehead, Jermaine Turner, Chris Hawkins, Kyle Demas, Sean Santana and none other than rookie phenom, Marshall Phillip. Now, I don't know what street ballers they have, but I don't think any of them can beat those guys."

"Hey, I know one" yelled Joe.

Since I was now committed, I had to practice like there was no tomorrow. Luckily Vann and Kevin paced me on the track. They helped me practice my dribbling and spinning moves all around the track.

"Come on, now. It's gotta be faster than that. Push the ball in front of you. Let's go," Vann used to exhort me all the time.

"Man, the hell with this. What makes pops know so much? Who is he? He never played in the league – who the hell is he?" Asked a very out of breath Kevin one fine day.

Who was Mr. Vann?

It took us a long time to piece together Vann's life story. We found out about it in flashes or whenever the old man was feeling particularly garrulous.

How Vann and his mother used to wait for the man of the house all the time. How little Vann never went to sleep till he saw his papa. But Vann' father never had any time for them. He was a good player. A great one, in fact, and he never forgot it, nor did he let anyone forget it either.

Even outside his home, he would kiss other women in front of his wife and kid, not caring that they saw, not caring that the whole world saw him. He thought he was on top of the world.

One day, his mom could not handle it anymore. "When is this gonna stop?" she asked him.

"All this coming home drunk, all the women. You think you're a good role model for Vann junior."

"The hell with him. I didn't want you to have him anyway," said Vann's father. While Vann junior, our Vann, listened at the door, crying his heart out.

Mom was very angry. She grabbed her husband. But instead, he just turned around and starts slapping and kicking her. "Don't ever touch me," he yelled like a possessed man as he rained down blow after blow on Vann's mom. Vann junior ran out to stop Vann senior from beating his Mom. Vann senior slapped Vann junior in the head and kicked him to the floor before walking out of the house.

Mom hugged him and said, "Don't ever be like that, don't ever be like that. That is not a man, be better than him. Be a better man. No matter what you do in life, respect and help people. From star basketball player to a bum on the street, always help people boy, that's what a man does"

"Yes, Mommy," Vann Junior had made a promise that he kept for the rest of his life.

The Here and Now

"None of this yelling stuff is gonna help you in the games," Kevin told me. "Games, what the hell you talking about, boy?

"What, you didn't even tell him?" Keven stares at me. "Boy, you always want to be doing something else. Let's go. Spins, come on, spin," Vann said. I shrugged and continued with the practice.

The days seemed to fly by as the tournament came closer and closer. I continued my practice with tremendous passion. Meanwhile, Marshall became very fond of doing interviews on television talk shows.

"That's why we're in the league and they're not. Them cats ain't disciplined enough to be here. Trust me, no streetballer is gonna beat me. They're not smart enough and they're definitely not nice enough," he told the sports announcer, who went his usual "you heard it here first" spiel.

As for me, I practiced so hard that I could hear Vann voice in my dreams going, "Dance, come on, dance with the rock," even as I slept with my little sister on my back.

The Night before the Tournament

I found myself sitting with old man Vann on the park bench. "So, tomorrow, it's all or nothing, eh."

"Yep, something like that," I replied. "Just don't be too cool," said Vann.

"Eh, what?" I did not get it.

"Yeah, that's what all the yelling was about…enthusiasm. Don't be too cool, let that dog inside you come out for once, then let's see how the boys try to handle you." As I nodded my head in affirmation, Vann merely said, "I'll be waiting, boy."

Chapter Thirteen

○ The Day of the Great Game!

I remember the day of the great game as clearly as yesterday. As I was getting dressed, little Brooklyn sat on the bed watching me. "You ready?" I asked her. She nodded her head. I placed her on her usual place on my shoulders and went downstairs.

Even from this distance, I could hear all the noise from the court that had been custom-built for the tournament. Kevin and Vann were waiting for me. I smiled and waved to them. "Damn, I thought I would have a little more of a crowd to walk me in," I said.

"Nah, brother. No one thinks you can win. It's just me, Pops, you, and the little one," said Kevin pointing towards Brookes on my shoulder.

There was something that has left me perplexed for quite some time. I eventually decided to come right up front after setting Brookes down. "Can I ask you a question?" I asked both Joe and Kevin. "What's up?" said Kevin.

"Why did you help me out like this? Why have you been hanging out with me? I'm just another cat that didn't make it, right?" I asked. Kevin looked at me like he was all confused. "Sit down for a second," he said as he stopped me on our way to the court.

"We were in the 10th grade and there was a long line to play Takin, so I came in the store and set my quarters on the machine," said Kevin.

"Yea, we always used to do that." I smiled in recollection.

"Yea, I did the same to let people know I had the next turn. Anyway, Greg Springer came in and just suckered me and took my quarters and put it in the machine. Now, you remember how big G was?"

I nodded my head, "Hell yeah!"

Kevin took a deep breath and continued, "Anyway, I stepped up to him and although he was much bigger than me, his boy was gonna jump me. And you stepped up and were like – 'Nah, it ain't going down like this. First of all, you all not gonna jump shorty here and second he had next.' When you said that, I mean, damn, Darren Drake stepped up for me. Everyone listened to you man."

"Oooohhh, I remember that. That was you, eh?" I asked Kevin. He nodded his assent.

"Bro. You helped me when you didn't have to. I mean, it was timing – you could help me, and you did, with no strings attached. Now, you a little down and out, and my brother is doing his thing and I can help you. No strings attached. Everything in this world is about timing –right place and the right time," he finished. I stood up from the chair and gave him a hug.

My trust in people that had taken such a severe turn for the worse after Marshal just went up a notch was restored. "Thanks, man," I said, my voice thick with emotion.

"It's nothing. Just go out there and drag whoever is in front of you," said Kevin. "What about you, coach? You know so much about the game. Did you ever play?" I asked Vann.

"Nah, but my father did and…" Vann stopped midsentence. "And what?" prompted Kevin.

"And nothing. In fear that I would be just like my dad, I never played the game I love." Vann replied. At that time, we were a long way away from knowing his full story, so I went "What? but that's crazy?"

"Yep, all I ever did was practice and study the game from books and watching TV. All because of my fears. I let my fears run my life." He said a single tear ran down his face. I hugged him as well. Whatever happened on the court today, these people were my lifeline, my team, and my support system – all rolled into one.

"Just destroy whoever is standing in front of you, as shorty said," said Vann gesturing to Kevin who was trying to keep pace with our long strides. We started walking towards the tournament. I picked Brooklyn and put her back on my shoulders. "Let's rock," I said and meant it too.

I cut through the crowd as I used to in the past. "So, this is where my story started. Me and my best friend, huh? Well, there's no more time to talk, just time to get at him for everything. Payback time!" I thought to myself.

I walked onto the caged court with my usual cool swagger. I could see Vann and Kevin standing right outside the cage. Vann was yelling last-minute instructions. "Alright, mister cool, you better toughen up or these kids will whip you!" I positively strutted by the gate where Vann and Kevin were standing. I smiled at them. Kevin jumped up and down, all hyped up. "That's my boy! Let's go, baby!" he yelled.

"Ok, ok. This is definitely the game of the day. Not just because it's a million bucks at stake but because these two men have a history with each other," went the game announcer.

The game announcer looked at me and asked me. "You want to tell me what's up with you two?"

I looked at Marshall with a very serious look on my face. "I have seen him on TV a couple of times, but...no I don't know him," I said shaking my head.

"What about you?" The game announcer asked Marshall who just laughed, and said, "This scum ball used to carry my bags in high school and college."

This...This thing I used to call a friend. . I had killed for him, risked a lifelong jail term for him!

Meanwhile, the crowd started hooting, yelling, and laughing. They were like the crowds who used to throng the arenas in ancient Rome, baying for fresh blood. They wanted to see me beaten and humiliated for daring to challenge one of their great idols. They wanted to see me pushed into the dirt.

○ Who will Win the Game?

"Ok baby let's get this started," said the game announcer. Meanwhile, Marshall, the ever-consummate showman walked around banging on the gates so that he could get the crowd more hyped up. It worked except for Kevin who yelled, "Please, you're weak."

Meanwhile, the referee pulled out a quarter out and looked at Marshall. "Call it."

I looked him in the eye. "Nah, let him get the rock first," said Marshall knowing the crowd was hanging on to his every word.

"It's like that? Ok. You guys know the rules. The game is 22, or five minutes, whichever comes first. No fighting or you're gone. May the best man win," said the ref in the mike to the accompanying roar of the crowd.

The game started really fast. There is no doubt that he was good. Damn good. I tried to dribble but Marshall stepped in close and stole the rock. As he went to the basket, he faked and took me completely by surprise. As I flew past, he scored. Needless to say, the crowd went crazy. But I was not unduly worried. I had plenty of time. I deliberately put a very nonchalant look on my face, as if I did not have a single care in the world.

However, Vann looked very upset, especially since Marshall took possession of the ball like taking cotton candy from a child. He did his patented dribble move and stepped back and hit a jump shot that soared gracefully and went into the basket. The crowd went wild.

"What, what? I told you I couldn't lose. I told you," he crowed at me. "This boy is soft," he yelled to the crowd. "Let's go, baby! Let's go!"

Kevin moaned in agony. He really thought it was all over for me. I tried to take the ball from him, but he stepped back real fast and hit a two-pointer. "Bang, Bang. Put your hands up, son. Come on, son," he goaded me.

"Pull your head out of your backside boy!" Vann yelled from the crowd.

I tried to block him, but he took the ball again. As he tried to get past me, I adroitly stole the ball from under his nose and tried to score but he elbowed me out of the way. I hit the gate very hard and start bleeding from right above my eye. I could not see and fell down to the ground.

Kevin muttered a string of expletives at Marshall. "Don't get beat down. Please don't leave this court and get whipped," he yelled at me. Marshall laughed at Kevin. "What's up, Darren? You finally got a girl?" He said pointing towards Kevin.

"Wake up boy! And play this game with your heart. Your heart boy!" Vann yelled at me. I got up and walked to the top of the key, dripping blood all the way. "That's why the game is nothing. Now everyone wants to be too cool," Vann started mumbling and yelling at the same time.

I could not blame him for his distress. After all, I was in serious trouble. I could not see properly, and my opponent had me outfoxed every step of the way. In the eyes of the crowd, it was all over and I don't blame them since I was fumbling and weaving around like a drunken man.

"How do you win, boy? With your heart!" I heard Vann yell at me.

Marshall checked the ball up. I did a quick cross-
over move that lost Marshall. "Oh no baby, he
didn't go that way," sang out Vann.

I reached the basket and jumped. Marshall tried to
block the shot and we banged into each other. I
took the hit and still managed to dunk as well.
"Awww!!!" I yelled. Outside the gate, Vann started
yelling at me. "Awww, here he is! Brooklyn's
Lochness monster has awoken. Let's go now!"

"Where I'm From," by Anthony Hamilton starts
playing as the game swung back and forth. But I
kept scoring and scoring. I tried to back Marshall
down and he threw me out of the way. Marshall
stole the ball and went in for the dunk. Then he
went over to where Vann and Kevin were sitting
and yelled "Yesssssss" at them.

The game continued to rest on a razor's edge. The
score was 21 to 20 with Marshall in the lead. There
were only seven seconds left.

The Final Countdown!

I remember that time as if it was a dream. I was
detached from my body and looking on as a
bystander as the game continued in front of me.
Everything happened in slow motion after that.

Not just my future, but the future of my baby sis also depended on these few seconds. It was time for me to right all the wrongs that Marshall had done to me. To give us a better future. To take my place under the sun.

There was blood dripping from my eye. I started jab stepping and Marshall played deep defense. It made sense since he was already in the lead and just needed to hold on for a few seconds. I looked at the clock. There were only four seconds left. Four seconds to turn my whole life around!

I dribbled forwards and stepped back just when I was about to shoot the two. Marshall jumped out at me. I faded away and took the shot. I fell and Marshall landed on top of me.

The ball was going in slow motion through the air and then... right into the net.

The band on my wrist said RESPECT.

I was on the ground, watching the shot go in the hoop. I was only looking at the shot with one eye and blood was pouring out of the other. The buzzer went off. Kevin cheered and was jumping up and down. Vann was clapping and tears were rolling down his eyes.

I looked over at Vann from the ground. He got up and started yelling like crazy. They opened the gate and my sister was suddenly in my arms. The crowd was going wild. In slow motion, Brooklyn leaned over and kissed me on the eye that had a cut over it. I don't remember anything beyond that point.

Epilogue

It has been five months since that day when I scraped victory from the jaws of defeat. I am now a hotshot shooting guard at BSU. I was in my new million-dollar house with my foul weather friends Kevin, and Vann when I heard the sports announcer.

"This just in…Marshall Phillip was in a very brutal car wreck. While the NBA star is alright, he may never be able to play basketball again."

"Karma," said Vann and walked away.

"Damn, I wish him the best," Said Kevin.

I am now a really big star and there's no sports magazine that doesn't display my name and face on the front page. I am called the "Rookie sensation of the NBA."

One day as I was driving downtown with Kevin, he said, "You know what I wanted to tell you? I heard your boy Marshall is back in the hood with his mom. I heard he's out there bad."

"Damn," I said as I thought about my next move. I knew what I had to do. The next evening, I knocked on an apartment door. "Coming…" I heard Patricia. "Oh my God!" she said as she opened the door to me.

Marshall was sitting on the couch with his leg up. I walked over to where Marshall was sitting. "What's up, boy?" I asked him.

"Mr. NBA. What you come over here for? What you want?" He asked me while looking surprised.

"I heard you were back in the hood nigga, so I knew that it couldn't mean anything good."

"So, what you come to rub it in? Oh haha! Marshall's back, living with his crackhead mommy." He said bitterly. "Naah, it's not like that," I dropped a bag on the floor. Marshall leaned over and opened the bag. It was full of money.

"What's this?" he asked as I started walking towards the door.

"Something so you can get your mom outta here. You know, you deserve a better life than this," I replied.

The tears were running freely down Marshall's face. "You know I'm still the best, I was always better than you."

"Oh yea, I almost forgot," I opened up the gym bag I was carrying and took out the MVP trophy that Marshall's mother's boyfriend had pawned when we were younger.

"Where'd you get that?" he asked looking fervently at it.

"Our mom...I mean, my mom went and bought it back from the pawnshop after everything happened that night." By now Patricia was also trying unsuccessfully to silence her sobs.

"Anyway, take care of yourself," I said before they could see my tears. I left them right there as I got into my Porsche. I looked into the mirror and smiled as Glen Lewis's "Don't you Forget It" played in the background. I looked in the mirror, smiled, and sped off into the sunset...

WITH APPRECIATION AND GRATITUDE

I would like to thank the Lord Jesus Christ for without him all that I have been able to achieve would not have been possible.

I want to thank my mother for teaching me what hard work truly means and giving me my unstoppable attitude.

Special thanks to my mentor, my friend Mr. Theodore Vann for showing me how and what it means to be a leader, and strong educated black man in America and for giving me the inspiration for this book.

And finally, thank you Gayle Kurtzer-Meyers for the assistance in making this happen. You are appreciated.

Made in the USA
Middletown, DE
09 January 2020